Hitopadesha
Tales

An imprint of Om Books International

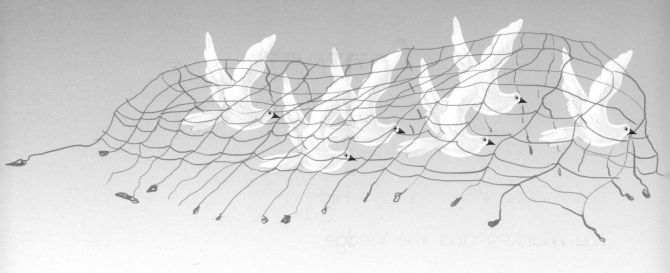

Reprinted in 2016 by

An imprint of Om Books International

Corporate & Editorial Office
A 12, Sector 64, Noida 201 301
Uttar Pradesh, India
Phone: +91 120 477 4100
Email: editorial@ombooks.com
Website: www.ombooksinternational.com

Sales Office
107, Ansari Road, Darya Ganj, New Delhi 110 002, India
Phone: +91 11 4000 9000
Fax: +91 11 2327 8091
Email: sales@ombooks.com
Website: www.ombooks.com

Copyright © Om Books International 2012

Content: Subhojit Sanyal
Illustration: Braj Kishor, Sijo John, Jithin

ISBN : 978-93-81607-64-0

Printed in India

10 9 8 7 6 5 4 3 2

Contents

The Hunter and the Doves

Once upon a time, on the banks of the Godavari river, there was a huge silk-cotton tree. It was home to a large flock of doves. Every evening, the doves would all come back to the silk-cotton tree and rest through the entire night. The next morning, they would once again fly away from there in search of food.

One morning, the entire flock of doves left from the silk-cotton tree in search of food. They kept flying for a while, when suddenly one of them cried out, "Did you see that? There are rice grains scattered all over the ground there. We are so lucky! Food, lots and lots and lots of food."

However, the king of the doves was not satisfied. "That is indeed very strange," he declared.

"Grains of rice in an uninhabited place! This could be a trap by some evil hunter."

"Oh please do not stop us!" pleaded his subjects. "As you can see there is nobody down there. Let's just fly down and eat a hearty breakfast!"

The king agreed to what was being proposed and the doves all came down to the ground to eat the rice grains.

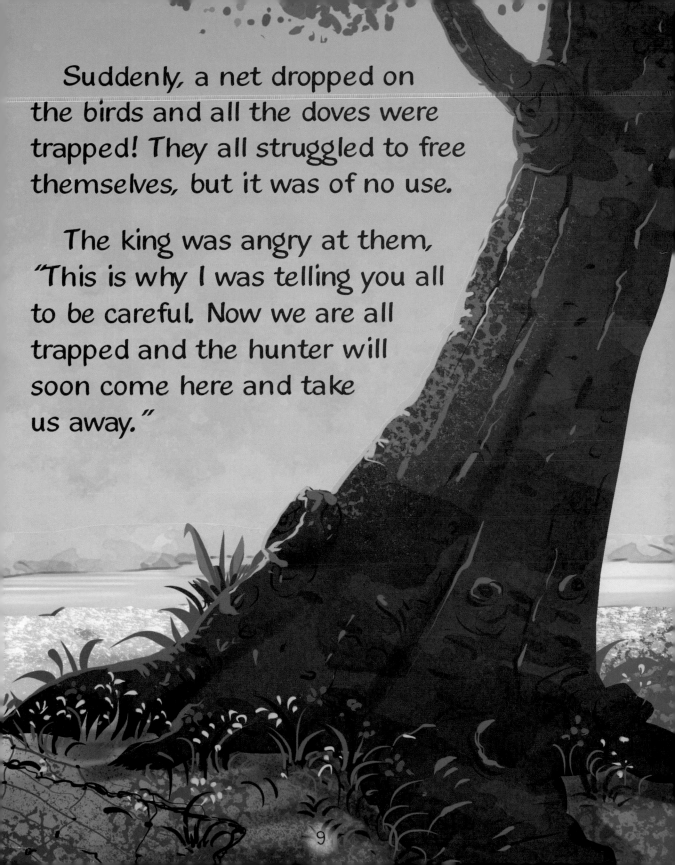

Suddenly, a net dropped on the birds and all the doves were trapped! They all struggled to free themselves, but it was of no use.

The king was angry at them, "This is why I was telling you all to be careful. Now we are all trapped and the hunter will soon come here and take us away."

And the king of the doves was indeed right. The hunter who had set this trap came towards the doves and said, "Ah, my foolish birds! Thanks to you, I have had quite a good catch today."

Just as the hunter was getting ready to pick up the net with all the doves caught

in it, the king of doves told his subjects, "Quick! We must all grab hold of the net and start flying upwards. That is the only way in which we can save ourselves."

The other doves did not question their king again and did as they were told. Each dove grabbed a portion of the net, wriggled out their wings and together, they all started flying upwards, in one direction.

The hunter looked on in shock, as the entire flock of doves flew away from him, with his net. "Come back here... you all are mine! Wait, I shall catch you as soon as you get back on land."

Even though the hunter chased after the doves, he couldn't keep up with them for too long and had to stop, huffing and puffing.

One of the doves then asked his king, "Now that we have managed to run away from the hunter, what are we going to do about the net?"

The king thought about it for a while and then said, "Let us go back to the silk-cotton tree. My friend, the mouse, lives in a hole in the tree trunk and he will help cut this net from over us."

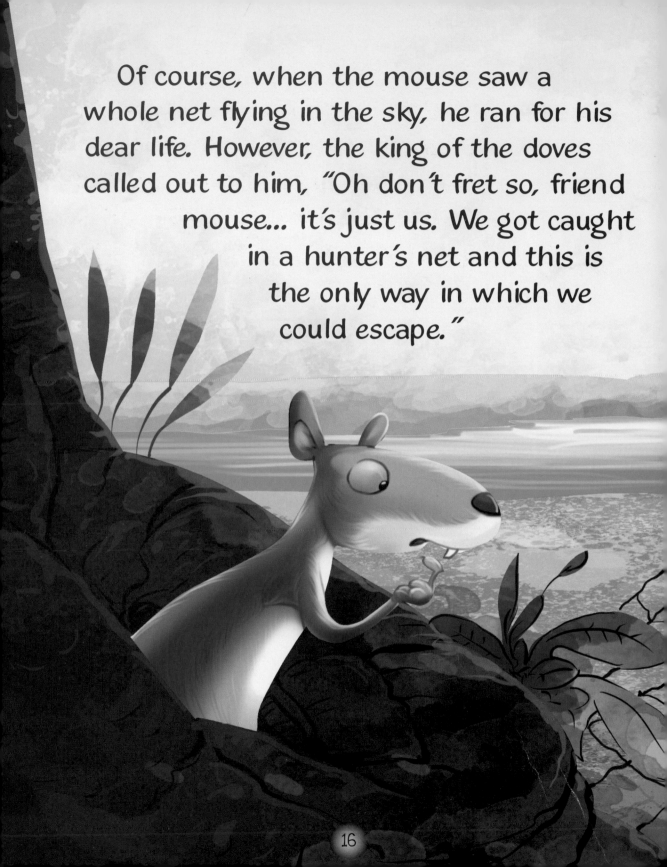

Of course, when the mouse saw a whole net flying in the sky, he ran for his dear life. However, the king of the doves called out to him, "Oh don't fret so, friend mouse... it's just us. We got caught in a hunter's net and this is the only way in which we could escape."

On recognizing his friend's voice, the mouse came back and looking at the doves he said, "Ah, I see that you all have been able to save yourselves because you all worked as a team! Don't worry now, I'll get you out of the net."

So saying, the mouse got busy nibbling at the net and soon the doves were all free. From that day onwards, the doves never went down to eat any scattered rice grains. And they always listened to their wise king!

Moral: Unity is strength.

The Mouse Who Jumped High

In the small town of Champaka, there lived a holy man. He would go around the town all day and people would give him food in his alms bowl. In the evening, after finishing his meal, the holy man would hang his alms bowl with the leftovers, high on a nail in the wall.

Now, a clever little mouse took note of this and began to steal the holy man's food from the bowl every day! The holy man tried many times to beat the mouse with his stick but to no avail.

Then one day, the holy man's friend came to pay him a visit. However, the holy man could not concentrate on his friend's stories, but instead kept a lookout for the mouse, hitting the bamboo stick on the ground to scare the mouse away.

"What is the matter?" asked the holy man's friend. "You look rather bothered. Is there something troubling you?"

The holy man, abashed, replied, "I apologize for not concentrating on what you were saying. You see, there is this mouse who has been stealing all the food that I manage to save!"

The holy man's friend looked at the high nail where the begging bowl was hanging

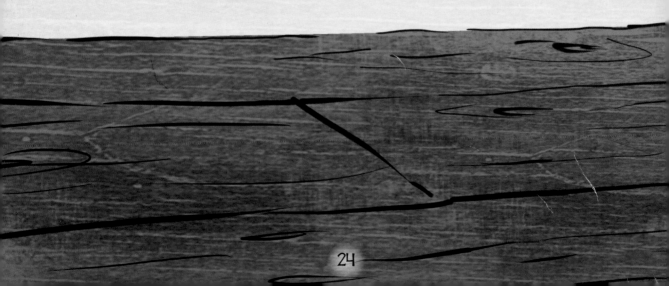

and said, "But that is incredible! This mouse must be able to jump quite high. How does he do it?"

The holy man thought for a while and said, "The only reason I can think of is that the mouse must have managed to store quite a lot of my food. And because of this, he now has the ability to make such a high jump."

The holy man and his friend at once began searching for the mouse's hidden stash of food and as soon as they found it, they dug it up and took it all away.

When the mouse went to collect some of the food he had stolen and stored, he saw that every single grain had been taken away from there. He realized that the holy man was now wise to his plans and therefore, he ran away from there and was never seen near the holy man's house again.

The Monkey and the Wedge

There was a great hullabaloo in the city of Varanasi. The construction of a new temple was in progress and there were a lot of carpenters working to build the temple.

One of the carpenters was in charge of sawing the logs into two halves. As he started work on a new log, his friend came and said, "It is getting quite late. Why don't we first go and eat our lunch. We can then come back and finish our work."

The log-cutting carpenter agreed at once
and putting a wedge in between the portion
of the log he had already sawed, so that the
two halves stayed apart, he went away with
his friend to eat his lunch.

No sooner was he gone from there than a group of monkeys arrived and started playing with the carpenter's tools. One of them went over to the still uncut log and started to play there.

Suddenly, his eyes fell on the wedge that was separating the cut part of the log and he got very interested in the wedge. He wondered why it had been kept in between the cut portion of the huge log.

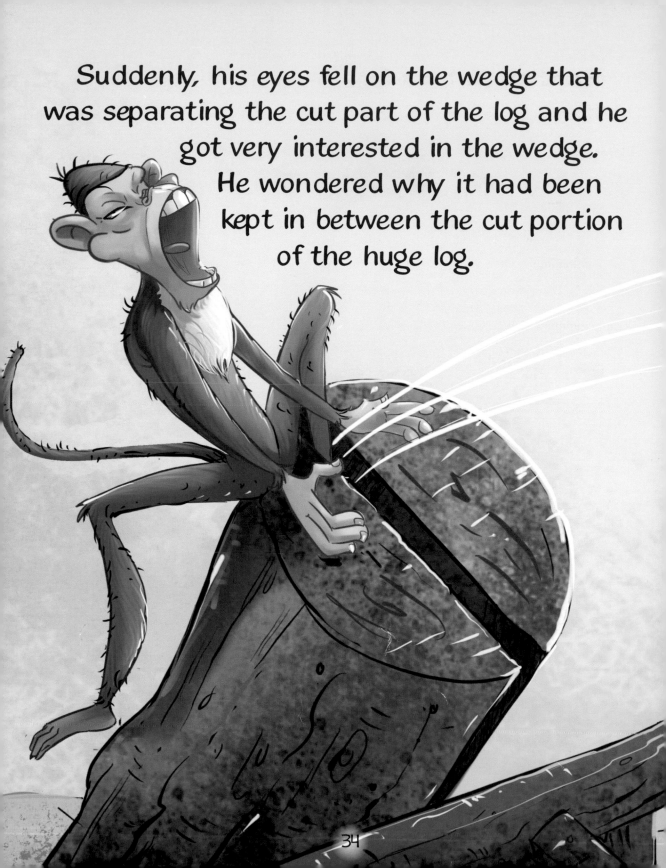

He then put his legs on either side of the cut log and started to pull at the wedge. It was stuck very tightly within the log and it did not come out at once.

So the monkey pulled at it with greater force. Suddenly, the wedge became loose and came out of the log. However, with the wedge coming out, the log at once slammed shut and the monkey's leg got stuck in the log!

It was quite some time before the monkey could free his leg, which was badly injured. His friends came running to his aid and they helped carry him away, since he could not walk by himself.

From that day onwards, the monkey never bothered with things that he did not know or understand.

Moral: Never play with things you do not understand.

The Poor Donkey

Once upon a time, in the city of Kasi, there lived a washerman. The washerman had a dog as his pet, and also a donkey, on whom the washerman would take his clothes to the bank of the Ganga to wash them.

One night, as the washerman was fast asleep, a thief entered his house. The thief started taking everything that he could lay his hands on.

The donkey who was still awake and standing right outside, saw the thief inside the house. He at once tugged at the dog who was sleeping right next to him, and said, "Wake up, my friend! There is a thief in the house!"

The dog shuffled in his position and replied, "So what? Just go back to sleep!"

The donkey was shocked to hear the dog speak thus and he scolded the dog, "What is the matter with you? Isn't it your job to wake up the master in such a situation?"

The dog was now irritated with the donkey's words and retorted, "And now you, a donkey, is going to explain my duties to me? Look here, the master has not been feeding me well at all for the last few days. So therefore, I too am not going to bother waking him up."

"Is this any time to complain this way?" shouted the offended donkey. "You can tell the master about this later, but first go and wake him up. Otherwise the thief will get away!"

The dog yawned and replied, "Let it be! Our master needs to be taught a lesson!" And so saying, the dog went back to sleep.

The donkey was quite angry with the dog's behaviour and replied, "Fine, do what you want. But I will not sit here and let this thief take what belongs to my master!" And the donkey started braying loudly.

The thief, on hearing the donkey bray like that, immediately went and hid in one corner of the house. The washerman too got up on hearing the donkey scream and started looking around to see if anything was wrong.

Obviously, he did not spot the thief who was hiding, and so the washerman walked out to the courtyard and picking up a stick, he gave the donkey a sound beating.

The dog too woke up again, hearing all the noise. He had a hearty laugh when he saw the thief running away, unnoticed by the master, and the donkey howling in pain.

The poor donkey never again bothered with waking up his master in case a thief had managed to find his way into the washerman's house.

Moral: Be wise about your plans and actions.

The Lion, the Mouse and the Cat

There once lived a mighty lion in a huge cave in the forest. The lion was the king of the jungle and he was loved and respected by all his subjects.

However, a little mouse who lived in a small hole just outside the lion's cave troubled the lion a great deal. Every time the lion would fall asleep, the mouse would come out of its hole and nibble quietly at the lion's mane. This was his meal.

When the lion got up and saw what had happened to its wonderful soft mane, he naturally got very angry. Since then, the poor lion tried to catch the mouse many a time, but remained unsuccessful on every attempt.

Finally, the lion got fed up with the mouse's constant pranks and he decided to do something about it. He went to the village and purchased a cat for himself.

He fed the cat very well and in return, the cat kept guard over the lion whenever he went to sleep. The mouse, on seeing the cat standing next to the lion's head, was now very scared to come out of his hole and therefore, the lion's mane remained untouched by the mouse for the next few days.

Every time the lion would hear the mouse move about, trying to come out and eat his mane, the lion would immediately give something to the cat to eat. This prevented the mouse from coming out at all.

The mouse was so sad at not being able to nibble at the lion's mane, that he packed his bags and left the cave.

Now that the lion knew that the mouse was gone and that his mane was now safe, he stopped feeding the cat. After a few days, the cat realized that her services were sadly no longer required, and therefore, she too left to look for her food somewhere else.

Moral: One must adapt oneself quickly to changing situations to be valued.

The Donkey Who Looked Like a Tiger

A long time ago, in the city of Hastinapur, there lived a washerman called Vilasa.

Vilasa had a donkey, on whom he would carry his load of clothes every day.

Sadly, the donkey grew weaker and weaker with each passing day. It was not strong enough to carry the heavy load that Vilasa put on him anymore. Soon, it was pretty clear to Vilasa too that if he did not do something about feeding his donkey, then the poor animal would surely die.

However, Vilasa did not have much money to feed his poor hungry donkey nicely. He therefore, thought up of a plan to get his donkey food and yet not have to pay a single paisa out of his pocket.

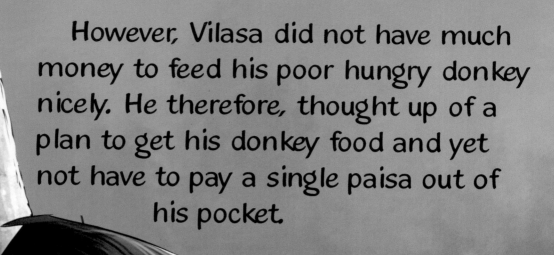

He wrapped the donkey in a tiger skin and then let him loose near a corn field that night. The farmer who owned the corn field saw a tiger coming towards his field from a distance. Naturally, he got very scared and ran away from there.

The donkey then had his fill of corns from the field and in a few days, he grew quite fat.

The poor corn field farmer lost all his crops to the so-called tiger that came to his fields every night. Unable to bear the losses anymore, the farmer sought the help of a hunter to help get rid of the 'tiger'.

That night, the hunter lay quietly in the fields, covering himself with a grey coloured blanket and waited patiently for the tiger to come to the field.

When it was indeed very late at night, the hunter saw some movement along the edge of the corn fields. It seemed to him that the tiger had arrived. The hunter immediately took his aim, waiting for the tiger to come closer so that he could shoot his arrows.

The donkey on the other hand, seeing the grey blanket from a distance, mistook it to be a girl donkey! Without even stopping to check carefully, the donkey started running towards the blanket, braying loudly all the while.

On hearing the donkey scream like that, the hunter was assured that he was indeed not a tiger, but a mere donkey. Therefore, just as the donkey came close enough to the hunter, the man pounced on him and gave him the beating of a lifetime.

Since then, the donkey never again wore a tiger's skin and went to eat in someone else's corn fields.

Moral: Never try to be something that you are not. Act according to the situation.

The Quail Who Didn't Run

It was during the festival dedicated to Lord Garuda, the King of all birds. The birds all declared that they would all go on a pilgrimage to the sea shore, as a mark of respect to their Lord.

Hearing this news, the quail turned to his friend, the crow, and said, "Don't you think we too should go on this pilgrimage?"

The crow replied at once, "Of course! It will be great fun. We'll all go with our friends and pay our respects to the Lord."

Therefore, as it was agreed upon by the two friends, the quail and the crow flew off towards the sea shore.

On the road, they noticed a herd of cows walking along their path, carrying bowls full of curd. The crow immediately went over to the quail and said, "Why don't we go and eat some of that curd? Those foolish cows will never even realize that we have eaten a portion away!"

The quail turned around and told the crow, "We are going on a pilgrimage for our Lord. How can you even think of committing a sin like thieving?"

The crow was not pleased with the quail's reply and said, "If you don't want to come, I have no problems. But do not tell me what I should do or not do."

The crow then immediately flew towards the cows and filled his beak with the delicious curd that one of them was carrying. He continued to do this for quite some time, when suddenly, that cow got suspicious.

She immediately warned her friends and they all placed their bowls on the ground and looked up to see who was stealing her curd. They spotted the crow and the quail flying above and came to the conclusion that they were both stealing curd.

The crow, on seeing the cows, knew that he was going to be in trouble. He quickly turned to the quail and said, "Come on, my friend, run!"

However, the quail replied, "You were the thief, not me. Why will they harm me then?"

The crow knew that he had
no time to argue with his friend,
therefore he declared, "Suit yourself!
I am flying away!"

And so saying, the crow flew away in full speed from there. The quail though kept sitting on the same branch where she had been perched.

Suddenly, a stone came and hit the quail. She looked around and saw that the cows were taking aim at her with more stones in their hands.

The quail tried to get away in a hurry on seeing this, but got hit by another stone before she was able to get away to safety. Since that day, the quail never met the crow again.

OTHER TITLES IN THIS SERIES

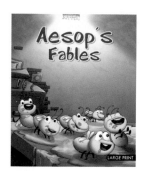 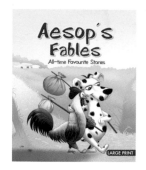  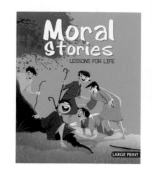

  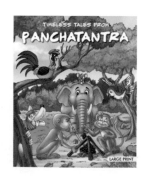 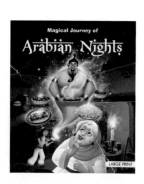